SUM

SUM

Forty Tales from the Afterlives

David Eagleman

PANTHEON BOOKS, NEW YORK

Library of Congress Cataloging-in-Publication Data

Eagleman, David.
Sum : forty tales from the afterlives / David Eagleman.
p. cm.
ISBN 978-0-307-37734-0
1. Future life—Fiction.   2. God—Fiction.   I. Title.
PS3605.A375S86 2008
813'.6—dc22
2008022071

www.pantheonbooks.com
Printed in the United States of America
First Edition
2   4   6   8   9   7   5   3   1

Contents

SUM

Sum

In the afterlife you relive all your experiences, but this time with the events reshuffled into a new order: all the moments that share a quality are grouped together.

You spend two months driving the street in front of your house, seven months having sex. You sleep for thirty years without opening your eyes. For five months straight you flip through magazines while sitting on a toilet.

You take all your pain at once, all twenty-seven intense hours of it. Bones break, cars crash, skin is cut, babies are born. Once you make it through, it's agony-free for the rest of your afterlife.

But that doesn't mean it's always pleasant. You spend six days clipping your nails. Fifteen months looking for lost items. Eighteen months waiting in line. Two years of boredom: staring out a bus window, sitting in an airport terminal. One year reading books. Your eyes hurt, and you itch, because you can't take a shower until it's your time to take your marathon two-hundred-day shower. Two weeks wondering what happens when you die. One minute realizing your body is falling. Seventy-seven hours of confusion. One hour realizing you've forgotten someone's name. Three weeks realizing you are wrong. Two days lying. Six weeks waiting for a green light. Seven hours vomiting. Fourteen minutes experiencing pure joy. Three months doing laundry. Fifteen hours writing your signature. Two days tying shoelaces. Sixty-seven days of heartbreak. Five weeks driving lost. Three days calculating restaurant tips. Fifty-one days deciding what to wear. Nine days pretending you know what is being talked about. Two weeks counting money. Eighteen days staring into the refrigerator. Thirty-four days longing. Six months watching commercials. Four weeks sitting in thought, wondering if there is something better you could be doing with your time. Three years swallowing food. Five days working buttons and zippers. Four minutes wondering what your life would be like if you reshuffled the order of events. In this part of the afterlife, you imagine something analogous to your Earthly life, and the thought is blissful: a life where episodes are split into tiny swallowable pieces, where moments do not endure, where one experiences the joy of jumping from one event to the next like a child hopping from spot to spot on the burning sand.

Egalitaire

In the afterlife you discover that God understands the complexities of life. She had originally submitted to peer pressure when She structured Her universe like all the other gods had, with a binary categorization of people into good and evil. But it didn't take long for Her to realize that humans could be good in many ways and simultaneously corrupt and mean-spirited in other ways. How was She to arbitrate who goes to Heaven and who to Hell? Might not it be possible, She considered, that a man could be an embezzler and still give to charitable causes? Might not a woman be an adulteress but bring pleasure and security to two men's lives? Might not a child unwittingly divulge secrets that splinter a family? Dividing the population into two categories—good and bad—seemed like a more reasonable task when She was younger, but with experience these decisions became more difficult. She composed complex formulas to weigh hundreds of factors, and ran computer programs that rolled out long strips of paper with eternal decisions. But Her sensitivities revolted at this automation—and when the computer generated a decision She disagreed with, She took the opportunity to kick out the plug in rage. That afternoon She listened to the grievances of the dead from two warring nations. Both sides had suffered, both sides had legitimate grievances, both pled their cases earnestly. She covered Her ears and moaned in misery. She knew Her humans were multidimensional, and She could no longer live under the rigid architecture of Her youthful choices.

Not all gods suffer over this; we can consider ourselves lucky that in death we answer to a God with deep sensitivity to the byzantine hearts of Her creations.

For months She moped around Her living room in Heaven, head drooped like a bulrush, while the lines piled up. Her advisors advised Her to delegate the decision making, but She loved Her humans too much to leave them to the care of anyone else.

In a moment of desperation the thought crossed Her mind to let everyone wait on line indefinitely, letting them work it out on their own. But then a better idea struck Her generous spirit. She could afford it: She would grant everyone, every last human, a place in Heaven. After all, everyone had something good inside; it was part of the design specifications. Her new plan brought back the bounce to Her gait, returned the color to Her cheeks. She shut down the operations in Hell, fired the Devil, and brought every last human to be by Her side in Heaven. Newcomers or old-timers, nefarious or righteous: under the new system, everyone gets equal time to speak with Her. Most people find Her a little garrulous and oversolicitous, but She cannot be accused of not caring.

The most important aspect of Her new system is that everyone is treated equally. There is no longer fire for some and harp music for others. The afterlife is no longer defined by cots versus waterbeds, raw potatoes versus sushi, hot water versus champagne. Everyone is a brother to all, and for the first time an idea has been realized that never came to fruition on Earth: true equality.

The Communists are baffled and irritated, because they have finally achieved their perfect society, but only by the help of a God in whom they don't want to believe. The meritocrats are abashed that they're stuck for eternity in an incentiveless system with a bunch of pinkos. The conservatives have no penniless to disparage; the liberals have no downtrodden to promote.

So God sits on the edge of Her bed and weeps at night, because the only thing everyone can agree upon is that they're all in Hell.

Circle of Friends

When you die, you feel as though there were some subtle change, but everything looks approximately the same. You get up and brush your teeth. You kiss your spouse and kids and leave for the office. There is less traffic than normal. The rest of your building seems less full, as though it's a holiday. But everyone in your office is here, and they greet you kindly. You feel strangely popular. Everyone you run into is someone you know. At some point, it dawns on you that this is the afterlife: the world is only made up of people you've met before.

It's a small fraction of the world population— about 0.00002 percent—but it seems like plenty to you.

It turns out that only the people you remember are here. So the woman with whom you shared a glance in the elevator may or may not be included. Your second-grade teacher is here, with most of the class. Your parents, your cousins, and your spectrum of friends through the years. All your old lovers. Your boss, your grandmothers, and the waitress who served your food each day at lunch. Those you dated, those you almost dated, those you longed for. It is a blissful opportunity to spend quality time with your one thousand connections, to renew fading ties, to catch up with those you let slip away.

It is only after several weeks of this that you begin to feel forlorn.

You wonder what's different as you saunter through the vast quiet parks with a friend or two. No strangers grace the empty park benches. No family unknown to you throws bread crumbs for the ducks and makes you smile because of their laughter. As you step into the street, you note there are no crowds, no buildings teeming with workers, no distant cities bustling, no hospitals running 24/7 with patients dying and staff rushing, no trains howling into the night with sardined passengers on their way home. Very few foreigners.

You begin to consider all the things unfamiliar to you. You've never known, you realize, how to vulcanize rubber to make a tire. And now those factories stand empty. You've never known how to fashion a silicon chip from beach sand, how to launch rockets out of the atmosphere, how to pit olives or lay railroad tracks. And now those industries are shut down.

The missing crowds make you lonely. You begin to complain about all the people you could be meeting. But no one listens or sympathizes with you, because this is precisely what you chose when you were alive.

Descent of Species

In the afterlife, you are treated to a generous opportunity: you can choose whatever you would like to be in the next life. Would you like to be a member of the opposite sex? Born into royalty? A philosopher with bottomless profundity? A soldier facing triumphant battles?

But perhaps you've just returned here from a hard life. Perhaps you were tortured by the enormity of the decisions and responsibilities that surrounded you, and now there's only one thing you yearn for: simplicity. That's permissible. So for the next round, you choose to be a horse. You covet the bliss of that simple life: afternoons of grazing in grassy fields, the handsome angles of your skeleton and the prominence of your muscles, the peace of the slow-flicking tail or the steam rifling through your nostrils as you lope across snow-blanketed plains.

You announce your decision. Incantations are muttered, a wand is waved, and your body begins to metamorphose into a horse. Your muscles start to bulge; a mat of strong hair erupts to cover you like a comfortable blanket in winter. The thickening and lengthening of your neck immediately feels normal as it comes about. Your carotid arteries grow in diameter, your fingers blend hoofward, your knees stiffen, your hips strengthen, and meanwhile, as your skull lengthens into its new shape, your brain races in its changes: your cortex retreats as your cerebellum grows, the homunculus melts man to horse, neurons redirect, synapses unplug and replug on their way to equestrian patterns, and your dream of understanding what it is like to be a horse gallops toward you from the distance. Your concern about human affairs begins to slip away, your cynicism about human behavior melts, and even your human way of thinking begins to drift away from you.

Suddenly, for just a moment, you are aware of the problem you overlooked. The more you become a horse, the more you forget the original wish. You forget what it was like to be a human wondering what it was like to be a horse.

This moment of lucidity does not last long. But it serves as the punishment for your sins, a Promethean entrails-pecking moment, crouching half-horse half-man, with the knowledge that you cannot appreciate the destination without knowing the starting point; you cannot revel in the simplicity unless you remember the alternatives.

And that's not the worst of your revelation. You realize that the next time you return here, with your thick horse brain, you won't have the capacity to ask to become a human again. You won't understand what a human is. Your choice to slide down the intelligence ladder is irreversible. And just before you lose your final human faculties, you painfully ponder what magnificent extraterrestrial creature, enthralled with the idea of finding a simpler life, chose in the last round to become a human.

Giantess

The afterlife is all about softness. You find yourself in a great padded compound. Everything appears designed for quietness and comfort. Your feet fall silently on the cushioned floor. The walls are pillowed. Echoes are dampened by foam ceiling tiles. A hard surface is impossible to find; feathers pad everything.

When you enter the grand hall, the first thing you notice is a sizable and princely man. He looks just as you might expect a god to appear, except that he is noticeably skittish and strained with worry around the eyes. He will probably be explaining that he is greatly disturbed by the nuclear arms proliferation on Earth. He says that he often awakens in a cold sweat with the sounds of colossal blasts hammering in his ears.

"To be clear," he says to you, "I am not your God. Instead, you and I are galactic neighbors; I am from a planet associated with the star you call Terzan Four. So we are all in the same mess."

"What mess?" you ask.

"Please don't talk so loudly," he softly admonishes. "For a long time we have been studying our neighbors: you Earthlings and thirty-seven other planets besides. We have developed highly accurate systems of equations to predict the future growth and social directions of your planets." Here he fixes your eyes. "It turns out that you Earthlings are among the least tranquil and content. Our predictions indicate that your weapons of war will grow increasingly loud. Your space exploration programs will produce thousands of noisy vessels that will thunder throughout the heavens with their deafening rocket propulsion. You Earthlings are like your explorer Cortez, standing atop a mountain peak and preparing to perturb every beach at all the lapping fringes of the Pacific."

"We're in a mess of expansionism?" you manage.

"That's not the mess," he hisses. "Allow me to illustrate the larger picture. You and I, our planets, our galaxy—we're part of what you should think of as an immeasurable living mass. You might call it a Giantess, but summarizing the concept in a word might give you the illusion that you can have a hint of a notion of her enormity.

"To give you a sense of scale, you are the size of an atom for her. Your Earth—sprouting with its untold layers of furiously fecund species—your Earth is tantamount to a single protein in the shadowy depths of a single one of her cells. Our Milky Way constitutes a single cell, but a small one. She consists of hundreds of billions of such cells.

"For millions of years, my people had no notion of her, just as a flatworm is unlikely to discover that the planet is round; a colony of bacteria will never know the walls of the flask; a single cell in your hand will not know it is contributing to a concerto on the piano.

"But with advancing philosophy and technology, we came to appreciate our situation. Then, a few millennia ago, it was theorized that we might be able to communicate with her. It was proposed that we might decipher her structure, deploy signals, influence her behavior in the manner that infinitesimal molecules—hormones, alcohols, narcotics— influence a creature like you.

"So we organized and educated ourselves. Instead of fretting through the doomed ignoble cycles of local politics, we dedicated our economy and sciences toward understanding the biochemistry of universal scales. We methodically mapped out the signaling cascades and stellar anatomy of her nervous system, and at last discovered how to transmit a signal to her consciousness. We sent a sharply defined sequence of electromagnetic pulses, which interacted with local magnetospheres, which influenced asteroid orbits, which nudged planets closer and farther from stars, which dictated the fate of lifeforms, which changed the gases in the atmospheres, which bent the path of light signals, all in complex interacting cascades we had worked out. Our calculations told us that it took a few hundred years for the transmission to arrive at her consciousness. At the time of the Arrival, I was sad to be traveling away from the planet while everyone was so excited to see what would happen."

His face twitches with painful trickles of reminiscence.

"But no one would have guessed what happened next: a great sheet of meteors rained down, incendiary hydrogen clouds crushed in, and these were followed by a multitude of black holes that mercilessly swallowed up the flying chunks and dust and the last light of remembrance. No one survived.

"In all probability, this was neutral to her. It might have been an immune system response. Or she might have been scratching an itch, or sneezing, or getting a biopsy.

"So we discovered that we can communicate with her, but we cannot communicate meaningfully. We are of insufficient size. What can we say to her? What question could we ask? How could she communicate an answer back to us? Perhaps that *was* her attempt to answer. What could you ask her to do that would have relevance to your life? And if she told you what was of importance to her, could you understand her answer? Do you think it would have any meaning at all if you displayed one of your Shakespearean plays to a bacterium? Of course not. Meaning varies with spatial scale. So we have concluded that communicating with her is not impossible, but it is pointless. And that is why we are now hunkered down silently on the surface of this noiseless planet, whispering through a slow orbit, trying not to draw attention to ourselves."

Mary

When you arrive in the afterlife, you find that Mary Wollstonecraft Shelley sits on a throne. She is cared for and protected by a covey of angels.

After some questioning, you discover that God's favorite book is Shelley's *Frankenstein*. He sits up at night with a worn copy of the book clutched in His mighty hands, alternately reading the book and staring reflectively into the night sky.

Like Victor Frankenstein, God considers Himself a medical doctor, a biologist without parallel, and He has a deep, painful relationship with any story about the creation of life. He has much to say about bringing animation to the unanimated. Very few of His creatures had thought deeply about the challenges of creation, and it relieved Him a little of the loneliness of His position when Mary wrote her book.

The first time He read *Frankenstein*, He criticized it the whole way through for its oversimplification of the processes involved. But when He reached the end He was won over. For the first time, someone understood Him. That's when He called for her and put her on a throne.

To understand His outpouring of feeling, you must understand the trajectory of God's medical career. God discovered the principles of self-organization by experimenting with yeast and bacteria. He reveled in the beauty of His inventions. Once He mastered the general principles, His inventions became increasingly sophisticated. With artistic flair He sewed together the astounding platypus, the compact beetle, the weighty woolly mammoth, the glistening pods of dolphins. His skills became razor-sharp and keen, and His accurate fingers fashioned—with blinding ambitious accuracy—all the animals at the limits of His vast imagination.

But then, unwittingly, He crossed His Rubicon. He created Man: His most prized possession, His treasure, pride, showpiece, and obsession.

Unlike the other animals, who experienced each day like the one before, Man cared, sought, yearned, erred, coveted, and ached—just like God Himself.

He marveled as Man picked through the ground and formed tools. The invention of musical instruments reached God's ears like a symphony. He watched with awe as men gathered up, erected cities, built walls. He felt His joy turn to trepidation as they began to scrap and brawl. It didn't take long before they were invading. Wars waged as He tried to talk sense to those who might listen.

He quickly discovered He had less control than He thought. There were simply too many of them. He tried to make good things come to good people, and bad to bad, but He didn't have the technology to implement it. The bloodshed mounted and was carried forward by the Assyrians and Babylonians; the Greco-Macedonians assailed their neighbors; the

Romans began their onslaught until the sieges of Barbarians and Goths. Byzantium rose and fell in blood; the Chinese baited and pounced; Europeans flung themselves at each other. The bright colors of His ground were darkening with Man's blood, and there was precious little He could do to stop it.

And all throughout, the voices of Man reached Him with pleas for help, entreaties for aid against one another. He plugged His ears and howled against the cries of pillaged villages, the prayers of exsanguinating soldiers, the supplications from Auschwitz.

This is why He now locks Himself in His room, and at night sneaks out onto the roof with *Franken-stein*, reading again and again how Dr. Victor Frankenstein is taunted by his merciless monster across the Arctic ice. And God consoles Himself with the thought that all creation necessarily ends in this: Creators, powerless, fleeing from the things they have wrought.

The Cast

Something dawned on you when you heard the children's song: *Merrily, merrily, merrily, merrily, life is but a dream*. You began to suspect that you were, perhaps, a butterfly dreaming it was a human, or, worse yet, a brain in a jar experiencing sights and sounds and smells and tastes—all of them but dreamstuff. And so you waited for death in order to wake up, in order to find out whether you were strapped with spotted wings or surrounded by a glass jar.

But it turns out you missed the mark. It is not life that is a dream; it is death that is a dream.

Stranger still, it is not your dream; it is someone else's.

You now recall that your dreams always had background characters: the crowds in the restaurant, the knots of people in the malls and schoolyards, the other drivers on the road and the jaywalking pedestrians.

Those actors don't come from nowhere. We stand in the background, playing our parts, allowing the experience to feel real for the dreamer. Sometimes we listen and pay attention to the plot of the dream. More often we talk among ourselves and wait for our shift to end.

This is not a job choice but indenture: you owe

the same number of hours of service as you spent dreaming during your lifetime. No one is very pleased about this work except for some former thespians among us. Mostly we give them the interactive roles every night; we're happy to sit in the background. If we're lucky enough that the dreamer casts us in a restaurant, we get a free meal out of it. On less fortunate nights, we're cast as masqueraders at a terrifying party, or as sufferers in deep circles of Hell, or as co-workers who have to point and laugh when the star walks in without clothes.

For those in the interactive roles, lines of dialogue are flashed on a screen behind the dreamer, to be delivered as convincingly as possible. Most of us give poor performances; we're not trained actors and have little incentive. Fortunately, the dreamers seem to believe whatever we deliver. Even if we don't look like the characters in question, the dreamers are convinced that we are who they think we are, and are only mildly confused even when we cast different genders in the roles.

Once, a long time ago, the dream casts went on strike, and for three days everyone on Earth dreamt of wandering empty homes and threading through deserted streets. Interpreting this as a grim omen, several people jumped to their deaths. When they showed up as new inductees in the dream cast, their piteous stories brought forth tears of sympathy from the others, who abandoned the strike immediately.

Perhaps it doesn't seem to you as if the afterlife is much of a punishment. But I haven't told you the worst part.

In the mornings, when we're done with our nighttime haunts in other people's skulls, we fall into restless slumbers of our own. And who do you think populates *our* dreams? Those who have finished their time here and pass from this world. We forever live in the dreams of the next generation.

The man to your left hypothesizes that everything is cyclical and that we'll eventually be back on Earth. This appears to be a time-sharing plan devised by some efficient deity; in this way we're not all populating the Earth at the same time.

What's the problem with this? There is a woman in my dreams whom I see every night, but I can never catch up with her, passing as we do into our next worlds.

Metamorphosis

There are three deaths. The first is when the body ceases to function. The second is when the body is consigned to the grave. The third is that moment, sometime in the future, when your name is spoken for the last time.

So you wait in this lobby until the third death. There are long tables with coffee, tea, and cookies; you can help yourself. There are people here from all around the world, and with a little effort you can strike up convivial small talk. Just be aware that your conversation may be interrupted at any moment by the Callers, who broadcast your new friend's name to indicate that there will never again be another remembrance of him by anyone on the Earth. Your friend slumps, face like a shattered and reglued plate, saddened even though the Callers tell him kindly that he's off to a better place. No one knows where that better place is or what it offers, because no one exiting through that door has returned to tell us. Tragically, many people leave just as their loved ones arrive, since the loved ones were the only ones doing the remembering. We all wag our heads at that typical timing.

The whole place looks like an infinite airport

waiting area. There are many famous people from the history books here. If you get bored, you can strike out in any given direction, past aisles and aisles of seats. After many days of walking, you'll start to notice that people look different, and you'll hear the tones of foreign languages. People congregate among their own kind, and one sees the spontaneous emergence of territories that mirror the pattern on the surface of the planet: With the exception of the oceans, you're traversing a map of the Earth. There are no time zones here. No one sleeps, even though they mostly wish they could. The place is evenly lit by fluorescent lights.

Not everyone is sad when the Callers enter the room and shout out the next list of names. On the contrary, some people beg and plead, prostrating themselves at the Callers' feet. These are generally the folks who have been here a long time, too long, especially those who are remembered for unfair reasons. For example, take the farmer over there, who drowned in a small river two hundred years ago. Now his farm is the site of a small college, and the tour guides each week tell his story. So he's stuck and he's miserable. The more his story is told, the more the details drift. He is utterly alienated from his name; it is no longer identical with him but continues to bind. The cheerless woman across the way is praised as a saint, even though the roads in her heart were complicated. The gray-haired man at the vending machine was lionized as a war hero, then demonized as a warlord, and finally canonized as a necessary firebrand between two moments in history. He waits with aching heart for his statues to fall. And that is the curse of this room: since we live in the heads of those who remember us, we lose control of our lives and become who they want us to be.

Missing

The debate about God's gender is misdirected. What we call God is actually a married couple. When they decided to create humans in their own image, they compromised and manufactured approximately equal numbers of both genders.

Each female She creates is close to Her heart. She becomes the woman for just a moment as She shapes her and, in this way, is able to try out different heights and weights, emotional depths and IQs, skin tones and eye colors. The same applies to every male shaped by Him. On certain nights when they're feeling liberal, each creates a member of the opposite sex, just to see what it's like.

When you die, you go to live in their large home and enjoy a parent-child relationship with them. Every human in the world is a child to them, and they devote tremendous effort to their parenting skills.

It is heartening to see that they learn from us in the same manner that all parents learn from their children. For example, it turns out they didn't know how to express the workings of their universe as equations, so they are greatly impressed with the ideas of their physicist children, who phrase clearly to them for the first time what they wrought.

On the other hand, it would be misleading to tell you that it's always been a happy family, because there was a period of time when that wasn't true. Their marriage was an arranged one, and over the millennia they grew unhappy with each other's company. By careful observation of their humans over the years, they learned that sometimes couples don't work out, that people separate, adulterate, divorce—and none of it is so terrible that the universe crashes down. And so, in the manner that all parents learn from their children, they separated.

There were many acts of bitterness. They stung each other with unfair accusations, using information so personal it shouldn't have been broached. Hurt, in an idea of quick revenge, She created a planet of all females. He retorted with a solar system of males. She encircled His line of planets with a band of women on meteors. The two of them armed the new humans to battle it out, women against men. Both sides were supplied with weapons ranging from sarcasm to tanks.

But something strange happened. The planets and meteors were silent. Orbits dragged like slow whispers through the empty space. No battles waged; not a shot was fired.

Upon close examination, they discovered that the monosexual inhabitants were miserable, crushed like existentialists under a feeling of the absence of something terribly important, something they couldn't put their fingers on.

Eventually, She dropped Her hands from Her hips and He from His. She spoke the first tender words in months, asking if He was hungry. He responded by offering to cook something for them both. The planets of men and women drifted back together, and the race started again, with its pursuits, seductions, choices, competitions, temptations, arguments, and a great cosmic sigh of relief as they all fell emancipated into each other's arms.

Spirals

In the afterlife, you discover that your Creator is a species of small, dim-witted, obtuse creatures. They look vaguely human, but they are smaller and more brutish. They are singularly unintelligent. They knit their brows when they try to follow what you are saying. It will help if you speak slowly, and it sometimes helps to draw pictures. At some point their eyes will glaze over and they will nod as though they understand you, but they will have lost the thread of the conversation entirely.

A word of warning: when you wake up in the afterlife, you will be surrounded by these creatures. They will be pushing and shoving in around you, rubbernecking, howling to get a look at you, and they will all be asking you the same thing: *Do you have answer? Do you have answer?*

Don't be frightened. These creatures are kind and innocuous.

You will probably ask them what they are talking about. They will knit their brows, plumbing your words like a mysterious proverb. Then they will timidly repeat: *Do you have answer?*

Where the heck am I? you may ask.

A scribe faithfully marks down your every word

for future record. Mother and daughter creatures peer out at you hopefully from observation decks.

To understand where you are, it will help to have some background.

At some point in the development of their society, these creatures began to wonder: *Why are we here? What is the purpose of our existence?* These turned out to be very difficult questions to answer. So difficult, in fact, that rather than attacking the questions directly, they decided it might be easier to build supercomputing machines devoted to finding the answers. So they invested the labor of tens of generations to engineer these. We are their machines.

This seemed a clever strategy to the elders of their community. However, they overlooked a problem: to build a machine smarter than you, it has to be more complex than you—and the ability to understand the machine begins to slip away.

When you wear out and stop functioning, your software is re-uploaded into their laboratory so they can probe it. This is where you awaken. And as soon as you make your first sound they crowd around you to learn one thing: *Do you have answer?*

They don't realize that when they dropped us into our terrarium, we didn't waste a moment: we built societies, roads, novels, catapults, telescopes, rifles, and every variety of our own machines. They have a hard time detecting this progress of ours, much less understanding it, because they simply can't follow the complexity. When you try to explain to them what has happened, they cannot keep up with your rapid and unfathomable speech, so they set about their dim-witted nodding. It makes them sad, and the most insightful among these creatures can sometimes be seen weeping in the corners, because they know their project has failed. They believe we have deduced the answer but are too advanced to communicate it at their level.

They don't guess that we have no answers for them. They don't guess that our main priority is to answer these questions for ourselves. They don't guess that we are unable, and that we build machines of increasing sophistication to address our own mysteries. You try to explain this to the creatures, but it is fruitless: not only because they don't understand you, but also because you realize how little you understand about our machines.

Scales

For a while we worried about a separation from God, but our fears were eased when the prophets revealed a new understanding: we are God's organs, His eyes and fingers, the means by which He explores His world. We all felt better about this deep sense of connection—we are a part of God's biology.

But it slowly grew clearer that we have less to do with His sensory organs and more to do with His internal organs. The atheists and the theists agreed that it is only through us that He lives. When we abandon him, He dies. We felt honored at first to be the cells that form God's body, but then it became clearer that we are God's cancer.

He's lost control of the small parts that constitute Him. We are dividing and multiplying. God and His doctors have tried to stanch the growth, the tumorous sprouting that makes His breathing difficult and endangers His circulation. But we're too robust. Throw storms and quakes and pestilence our way, and we scatter, regroup, and plan better. We become resistant and keep dividing.

He has finally reached His peace with this and lies quietly in His bed at the convergence of green antiseptic corridors.

Sometimes He wonders if we're doing it on purpose. Are His beloved subjects yearning to know His body, to metastasize throughout His greatness by way of His arterial system? He doesn't suspect that we're innocent of the journey.

Then He begins to notice something. While He cannot stop us or hurt us, there's something that can. He watches us turning to the smaller scales to battle our own leukemias, lymphomas, sarcomas, melanomas. He witnesses His subjects anointing themselves in chemotherapy, basking in the glow of radiation therapy. He watches His humans recklessly chewed up by the trillions of cells that constitute them.

And God suddenly bolts up in His bed with a revelation: everything that creates itself upon the backs of smaller scales will by those same scales be consumed.

Adhesion

We are the product of large beings that camp out on asteroids and call themselves Collectors. The Collectors run billions of experiments on the time scales of universes, subtly tuning the galaxy parameters this way and that, making bangs bigger and lesser, dialing fundamental physical constants a hair's breadth at a time. They are continually sharpening pencils and squinting into telescopes. When the Collectors have solved a problem that was formerly mysterious to them, they destroy that universe and recycle the materials into their next experiment.

Our life on Earth represents an experiment in which they are trying to figure out what makes people stick together. Why do some relationships work well while others fail? This is completely mysterious to them. When their theoreticians could not see a pattern, they proposed this problem as an interesting question to explore. And so our universe was born.

The Collectors construct lives of parametric experiments: men and women who adhere well but are shot past one another too briefly—brushing by in a library, passing on the step of a city bus, wondering just for a moment.

And the Collectors need to understand what men and women do about the momentum of their individual life plans, when in the rush and glare of the masses they are put together as they move in opposite directions. Can they turn the momentum of choices and plans? The Collectors sharpen their pencils against their asteroids and make careful study.

They research men and women who are not naturally adherent but are held together by circumstance. Those pressed together by obligation. Those who learn to be happy by forcing adhesion. Those who cannot live without adhesion and those who fight it; those who don't need it and those who sabotage it; those who find adhesion when they least expect it.

When you die, you are brought before a panel of Collectors. They debrief you and struggle to understand your motivations. Why did you decide to break off *this* relationship? What did you appreciate about *that* relationship? What was wrong with so-and-so, who seemed to have everything you wanted? After trying and failing to understand you, they send you back to see if another round of experimentation makes it any clearer to them.

It is for this reason only that our universe still exists. The Collectors are past deadline and over budget, but they are having a hard time bringing this study to a conclusion. They are mesmerized; the brightest among them cannot quantify it.

Angst

As humans we spend our time seeking big, meaningful experiences. So the afterlife may surprise you when your body wears out. We expand back into what we really are—which is, by Earth standards, enormous. We stand ten thousand kilometers tall in each of nine dimensions and live with others like us in a celestial commune. When we reawaken in these, our true bodies, we immediately begin to notice that our gargantuan colleagues suffer a deep sense of angst.

Our job is the maintenance and upholding of the cosmos. Universal collapse is imminent, and we engineer wormholes to act as structural support. We labor relentlessly on the edge of cosmic disaster. If we don't execute our jobs flawlessly, the universe will re-collapse. Ours is complex, intricate, and important work.

After three centuries of this toil, we have the option to take a vacation. We all choose the same destination: we project ourselves into lower-dimensional creatures. We project ourselves into the tiny, delicate, three-dimensional bodies that we call humans, and we are born onto the resort we call Earth. The idea, on such vacations, is to capture small experiences. On the Earth, we care only about our immediate surroundings. We watch comedy movies. We drink alcohol and enjoy music. We form relationships, fight, break up, and start again. When we're in a human body, we don't care about universal collapse—instead, we care only about a meeting of the eyes, a glimpse of bare flesh, the caressing tones of a loved voice, joy, love, light, the orientation of a house plant, the shade of a paint stroke, the arrangement of hair.

Those are good vacations that we take on Earth, replete with our little dramas and fusses. The mental relaxation is unspeakably precious to us. And when we're forced to leave by the wearing out of those delicate little bodies, it is not uncommon to see us lying prostrate in the breeze of the solar winds, tools in hand, looking out into the cosmos, wet-eyed, searching for meaninglessness.

Oz

At the outset of the afterlife you find a scroll that informs you, in the scrawl of an ancient scribe, that you now have the opportunity to meet the Creator of the universe—but only if you are among the most courageous. You wonder what magnitude of maker could require such bravery to be in His presence. You imagine a face larger than the orbit of the moon, a voice louder than a hundred blasts of Vesuvius, and you begin to suspect that your limited imagination is inadequate for the numinous experience in store.

You hear a thunderous booming voice in the distance, and your legs begin to shake. You look inward: *Am I brave enough to handle this?*

A great journey awaits. Along the way you face fears and conquer them, identify streams of self-doubt and ford them, discern the peaks of your arrogance and descend them, spot the clouds of self-pity that hang over you and hike out from under them. By the time the road ends, you emerge with renewed confidence—ready, you believe, to meet your maker, to face the face, to perceive a glimpse of the master-mind who crafted the masterpiece.

You approach the door of a great castle. Even now, the booming voice hanging over the landscape causes you to question: *Am I among the most brave? Do I possess what is required?* You throw your weight against the door, enter a grand foyer, and follow a hallway to a grand room.

And there you see the face. Indeed, it is larger than the moon's orbit. It is a sight beyond the pens of lyric poets. It is the ocean in its terrifying power and rhythmic grace. It is a face that looks like your father and like your mother; it commands the knowledge of a thousand scholars, the empathy of a thousand lovers, the mystery of a thousand strangers.

It is a face that makes the journey worthwhile. It is a face worthy of the master of the universe.

You quiver and shake, hypnotized, you in your cotton-mouthed ecstasy.

The volcanic voice booms forth, blowing back your hair. "Are you brave?"

"Yes," you stammer. "That's why I'm here."

The valleys of the lips curl a little, as though to laugh.

Then you hear an electrical buzzing sound. The face grows wavy with horizontal scanning lines and disappears in a flash of phosphors.

Nothing remains in the great space but a small yellow curtain where the face used to be. The curtain pulls back. A wrinkled hand pushes up glasses on the face of a wrinkled little man. He is gout-ridden, has a resting tremor, and a vialful of colorful pills. He is stooped. He is swaybacked and balding. You look at each other.

He says, "It is not the brave who can handle the big face, it is the brave who can handle its absence."

Great Expectations

As the happy result of a free-market capitalist society, we are finally able to determine our own hereafter. It has become privatized and computerized. For a reasonable price, you can download your consciousness into a computer to live forever in a virtual world. In this way, you can rage against the dying of the light by choosing an afterlife that is fast, furious, and spicy—the crystallization of your fantasies. You can predefine your lovers, maximize your sexual allure, zoom around electric pumping cities in your choice of a dozen Porsches. You get firmer muscles, a perfect complexion, and a flat washboard belly. Innumerable virgins cheerfully await your arrival. Cell phones and jet packs are standard issue. Sizzling cocktail parties run around the clock.

It is no surprise that everyone is lining up for this avant-garde afterlife. Instead of slipping into worm fodder, it is far better to choose the moment of your own death and elect the finest of all possible hereafters. The only ones not signing up are a few religious folks who claim they're waiting for their Heaven, imagining they will discover themselves in an afterlife of biblical description. The Company, having long ago outgrown the concept of God, attempts to explain to these people that their fantasies have cursed their available realities. The religious counter that God's greatest gift to them is the ability to look beyond what their eyes can see and have faith in something grander. That's not a gift, that's a trap, the Company retorts. It's like having a wonderful lover available but desiring an unattainable movie star instead. The religious don't sign up and eventually slip off into a neutral death in a lonely hospital bed.

For the rest of us, the transition into the virtual hereafter is painless: when your prescheduled moment arrives, you come in to the office and recline in the red dental chair. The Company nurse assures you that you will feel as though you've closed your eyes in their office and without delay opened them again in your glorious virtual afterworld. A technician presses a button and you become pulverized by a laser beam. A copy of the three-dimensional structure of your brain is re-created in zeros and ones on a cluster of hyperthreading processors.

There's only one caveat: the neuroscientists and engineers who have developed this procedure have no way of *proving* it works. After all, the pulverized have no way to report back. However, it is generally agreed that nothing can go wrong with the download: all of our physical theories predict that reconstructing an exact replica of the brain will reproduce exactly the feeling of being that person. So everyone presumes that it works.

Sadly, it does *not* work. Its failure is not due to bad engineers or unscrupulous businessmen, but instead stems from a misunderstanding of the cosmic scheme. Your essence cannot be downloaded because your essence (which the Company did not believe existed as a separate entity) gets spirited off to Heaven. Despite your excitement about your chosen afterlife, it turns out that God exists after all and has gone through great trouble and expense to construct an afterlife for us. So you awaken on soft clouds, encircled by harp-strumming angels, finding yourself swathed in a white toga.

The problem is that this isn't what you wanted. You've just paid good money for an afterlife of fast cars and charisma and drinking and lovemaking. This Heaven, by comparison, seems hopelessly inadequate and stale. You're wearing an ill-fitting white sheet instead of an antigravity jet pack. Endless white columns are the replacement for pumping electric cityscapes. There's manna and milk at the buffet instead of sushi and sake. The harp music is maddeningly slow. And you're still as unattractive as ever. There's nothing to do here. The overweight people to your left are playing bridge.

All this recent disappointment has put God in an awkward position. He nowadays spends much of His time trying to comfort His subjects scattered across the cloudscapes. "Your fantasies have cursed your realities," He explains, wringing His hands. "The Company offered you no evidence that it would work; why did you believe them?" Although He doesn't say it, everyone knows what He's thinking when He retires to His bed at night: that one of His best gifts—the ability to have faith in an unseen hereafter—has backfired.

Mirrors

When you think you've died, you haven't actually died. Death is a two-stage process, and where you wake up after your last breath is something of a Purgatory: you don't feel dead, you don't look dead, and in fact you are not dead. Yet.

Perhaps you thought the afterlife would be something like a soft white light, or a glistening ocean, or floating in music. But the afterlife more closely resembles the feeling of standing up too quickly: for a confused moment, you forget who you are, where you are, all the personal details of your life. And it only gets stranger from here.

First, everything becomes dark in a blindingly bright way, and you feel a smooth stripping away of your inhibitions and a washing away of your power to do anything about it. You start to lose your ego, which is intricately related to the spiriting away of your pride. And then you lose your self-referential memories.

You're losing you, but you don't seem to care.

There's only a little bit of you remaining now, the core of you: naked consciousness, bare as a baby.

To understand the meaning of this afterlife, you must remember that everyone is multifaceted. And since you always lived inside your own head, you were much better at seeing the truth about others than you ever were at seeing yourself. So you navigated your life with the help of others who held up mirrors for you. People praised your good qualities and criticized your bad habits, and these perspectives—often surprising to you—helped you to guide your life. So poorly did you know yourself that you were always surprised at how you looked in photographs or how you sounded on voice mail.

In this way, much of your existence took place in the eyes, ears, and fingertips of others. And now that you've left the Earth, you are stored in scattered heads around the globe.

Here in this Purgatory, all the people with whom you've ever come in contact are gathered. The scattered bits of you are collected, pooled, and unified. The mirrors are held up in front of you. Without the benefit of filtration, you see yourself clearly for the first time. And that is what finally kills you.

Perpetuity

If you wake up and find yourself in this suburb, you'll know you were a sinner. Not that the accommodations aren't nice; there are televisions here with many stations to choose from. You have neighbors on all sides of you, with whom you interact occasionally. There are shelves brimming with books that tell good but implausible adventure stories. The children here are sent to school, and the adults go to work. Careers are easy and the groceries are cheap.

You learn that this is called Heaven. We live close to God here. The only mysterious part is that all the good people you knew—the samaritans, the saints, the generous, the altruists, the selfless, the philanthropists—are not here. You inquire whether they have been sent on to a better place, a super-Heaven, but discover that these good people are rotting in coffins, the foodstuff of maggots. Only sinners enjoy life after death.

There have been many theories about why God would arrange things this way. Everyone has a hypothesis, and it's the customary topic of discussion at barbecue cookouts. Why are we the ones rewarded with an afterlife? It seems clear that God doesn't much like the inhabitants here; He rarely visits us. But He wants to make sure He keeps us alive.

The woman at the coffee shop insists He is keeping the bad ones around like the Romans kept gladiators: at some point we will fight to the death for His amusement. Your neighbor across the street theorizes that we are being stockpiled to wage war against another God in a neighboring universe, and only the sinful make useful soldiers.

But they're both wrong. In truth, God lives a life very much like ours—we were created not only in His image but in His social situation as well. God spends most of His time in pursuit of happiness. He reads books, strives for self-improvement, seeks activities to stave off boredom, tries to keep in touch with fading friendships, wonders if there's something else He should be doing with His time. Over the millennia, God has grown bitter. Nothing continues to satisfy. Time drowns Him. He envies man his brief twinkling of a life, and those He dislikes are condemned to suffer immortality with Him.

The Unnatural

When you arrive in the afterlife, the Technicians inform you of the great opportunity awaiting you: make any single change you want, and then live life over again. Their pamphlet suggests that you might choose to make yourself two inches taller, or give everyone on the Earth a better sense of humor, or make birds talk. You then get to rerun that choice on the Earth to see what happens. They inform you proudly that this is a unique experiential education program.

Having just attended your own funeral, you may be tempted to propose a clever choice: you want to be the one who eradicates death altogether from our planet.

Just be forewarned: if you propose this, a kind Technician may pull you aside to let you know that you have tried this path before in your previous reruns of life, and it inevitably led to frustration.

Are you telling me this because it will put you out of a job? you ask.

No, the Technician replies.

Is this because death is incurable? you ask.

No, the Technician says.

In that case I would like to have my wish fulfilled.

Suit yourself, replies the Technician.

So in your new life you grow into a famous medical visionary. You argue that there is no such thing as a natural death and raise millions to fund your research. You program computers to calculate all possible mutations of viruses before they happen and design prophylactic treatments against them. You compute the exact effects of every medication on the normal cycles of the body. Your aggressive anti-death program is a success: after the final breath of an incurably ill elderly woman, you are able to announce that hers represented the last natural death. Great celebrations ensue. People begin to live forever, healing just as they would when they were young, free at last from the overhanging cloud of mortality. You are greatly admired.

But eventually, just as the Technician warned, your success begins to lose its shine. People come to discover that the end of death is the death of motivation. Too much life, it turns out, is the opiate of the masses. There is a noticeable decline in accomplishment. People take more naps. There's no great rush.

In an attempt to salvage their once-dynamic lives, people begin to set suicide dates for themselves. It is a welcome echo of the old days of finite life spans, but superior because of the opportunity to say good-bye and complete your estate planning. That works well for a while, rekindling the incentive to live strongly. But eventually people begin to take the system with less than the appropriate seriousness, and if some large new development occurs, such as a new relationship, they simply postpone the suicide date.

Whole cadres of procrastinators grow. When they reschedule a new date, others ridicule them by calling it a death threat. There develops enormous social pressure to follow through with the suicides. At long last, after many abuses of the system, it is legislated that there is no changing a preset death date.

But eventually it comes to be appreciated that not just the finitude of life but also the surprise timing of death is critical to motivation. So people begin to set ranges for their death dates. In this new framework, their friends throw surprise parties for them—like birthday parties—except they jump out from behind the couch and kill them. Since you never know when your friends are going to schedule your party, it reinstills the carpe diem attitude of former years. Unfortunately, people begin to abuse the surprise-party system to extinguish their enemies under the protection of necrolegislation.

In the end, great masses of rioters break into your medical complex, kick the plugs out of the computers, and once again have a great celebration to mark the end of the last unnatural life, and you end up back in the Technicians' waiting room.

Distance

In the afterlife you find yourself in a beautiful land of milk and honey: there is no poverty, starvation, or warfare, only rolling hills and Lilliputian angels and evocative music. You discover that you are allowed to ask one question of your Maker.

You're led ceremoniously through the glistening arcades of the palace to the great hall, where your Maker sits enthroned in lights that hurt your eyes. You cannot direct your gaze fully at Him.

Nonetheless, you stand bravely in front of Him and ask, "Why do you live in a place like this, so far from Earth, instead of living down in the trenches with us?"

He is given pause by this question. Clearly no one has asked Him this in a long time. It is hard to tell in the bright light, but it looks as though His kind eyes well up.

He gazes wistfully out into the sky. "For a while I *did* live on Earth," He answers. "I was never one for exuberance, but nonetheless I had several homes in several countries. All my neighbors knew when I was there, and they would wave. I was well liked.

"I could run things well from that vantage— down in the trenches, as you say—and I actively enjoyed each acre of my creation by walking on it, smelling it, feeling the soil between my fingertips, living on it.

"But one day I came to one of my homes and found that all the windows had been broken."

He winces in reminiscence.

"Then that happened to a second one of my homes. I don't know who did it, or what their reasons were, but it dawned on me that the respect I once commanded was caving in. People began to cut me off in traffic. One morning I awoke to find people picketing in front of my driveway."

He falls silent, misty-eyed, contemplative.

You clear your throat. "That's when you came up here?"

"I came here for the same reason doctors wear uniforms of long white coats," He answers. "They don't do it for their benefit, but for yours."

Reins

First you notice there are many blunders: the good are going to Hell and the bad to Heaven. When you approach the woman at the front desk to inquire, you find she is recalcitrant and insolent. She tells you to go to line number seven, where you will fill out a complaint form and turn it in to desk number thirty-two. As you wait in line and strike up a conversation with the woman behind you, you discover that the afterlife was long ago given over to committees.

It turns out that power was wrested from God near the beginning, when he began to lose control of the workload. Humans began doing whatever they liked; adultery flourished, crime materialized and escalated. God realized that He had no concept of the skills required to run an organization of this magnitude. Because of the excessive procreation of His humans, the population was doubling at a blinding rate, and the managerial load for a hereafter became staggering. A file had to be kept on every individual, planet-wide, with constant updating of new sins and good deeds. God tried taking care of all this Himself, pushing through pencils so fast they smoked. Compounding the workload was the fact that God, in His bigheartedness, had also established pleasant after-lives for every animal. He grew exhausted but stated resolutely that He would not degrade His promises of afterlife. He would not abandon a single baby, a single animal, a single insect. He would not down-size. He had made His promises and intended to keep them.

The angels who had supported God in the begin-ning watched with concern as it seemed the whole operation might slip out of His control. They began to sow the seeds of discord, introducing the idea that God would never have gotten where He was without them. As the system grew progressively disorgan-ized, they hatched plans for their own rise to author-ity. As humans invented better technologies, the angels progressively took advantage of these to auto-mate the process. By the 1970s they were zipping through uncountable piles of punch cards; by the 1990s they had reduced the operation to a warehouse of computers; at the turn of the millennium they had constructed a sophisticated intranet by which they could track in real-time the disposition of all souls. God developed a reputation of being old-school, and the reins of power became increasingly slippery in His uneasy grasp.

Very few people visit Him anymore. He finds Himself lonely and misunderstood. He often invites over men like Martin Luther King, Jr., and Mahatma Gandhi, and together they sit on the porch drinking tea and lamenting about movements that sweep over the tops of their founders.

Microbe

There is no afterlife for us. Our bodies decompose upon death, and then the teeming floods of microbes living inside us move on to better places. This may lead you to assume that God doesn't exist—but you'd be wrong. It's simply that He doesn't know *we* exist. He is unaware of us because we're at the wrong spatial scale. God is the size of a bacterium. He is not something outside and above us, but on the surface and in the cells of us.

God created life in His own image; His congregations are the microbes. The chronic warfare over host territory, the politics of symbiosis and infection, the ascendancy of strains: this is the chessboard of God, where good clashes with evil on the battleground of surface proteins and immunity and resistance.

Our presence in this picture is something of an anomaly. Since we—the backgrounds upon which they live—don't harm the life patterns of the microbes, we are unnoticed. We are neither selected out by evolution nor captured in the microdeific radar. God and His microbial constituents are unaware of the rich social life that we have developed, of our cities, circuses, and wars—they are as unaware of our level of interaction as we are of theirs. Even while we genuflect and pray, it is only the microbes who are in the running for eternal punishment or reward. Our death is unnoteworthy and unobserved by the microbes, who merely redistribute onto different food sources. So although we supposed ourselves to be the apex of evolution, we are merely the nutritional substrate.

But don't despair. We have great power to change the course of their world. Imagine that you choose to eat at a particular restaurant, where you unwillingly pass a microbe from your fingers to the saltshaker to the next person sitting at the table, who happens to board an international flight and transport the microbe to Tunisia. To the microbes, who have lost a family member, these are the mystifying and often cruel ways in which the universe works. They look to God for answers. God attributes these events to statistical fluctuations over which He has no control and no understanding.

Absence

———

Heaven looked approximately like people said it would: vast gardens of flora and fauna, angels with harps, San Diego weather. But when you first arrived, you were surprised to find that everything was in disrepair. The gardens were vastly overgrown. The angels were gaunt, sitting on blankets with small paper cups for change in front of their dented harps. They tinkled out a small ditty as you walked by. The day was warm but the sky was gray with smog.

God is gone. The rumor is that He stepped out long ago, saying He'd be right back.

Some people hypothesize that God is never planning to return. Others say God went crazy; others assert He loves us but was called away to spawn new universes. Some say He is angry, others say He contracted Alzheimer's. Some hypothesize he is on siesta, others on fiesta. Some say God does not care; some say God cared but has passed away. Others suggest that it doesn't make sense to ask where He went, since He may never have been present. Perhaps aliens, not a god at all, built this place. Some ask whether we owe our afterlives to neutral scientific principles not yet understood. Others predict God is about to return at any moment; they point out that His days correspond to our millennia, and perhaps He's on an afternoon's drive.

Whatever lies behind His absence, it hasn't taken long for the garden to degrade into a Hobbesian jungle. People have belligerently taken sides based on their disappearance theories, and the debates rise like plumes of black smoke. At one point, someone found an old footprint of God's in a far reach of the garden and tried to carbon-date it, but no one agrees on the results.

Then an incredible thing happened. Someone started brawling, someone started shooting, someone started bombing, and now war has broken out on the consecrated plains of Heaven. New arrivals are swept directly into boot camp and trained in weaponry. The afterlife, as anyone here will tell you, is not what it used to be. We have ascended and brought the front line with us.

The new religious wars do not pivot on God's definition but instead on His whereabouts. The New Crusaders mount attacks against infidels who believe God is returning; the New Jihadis bomb those who don't believe that God has other universes to attend; the New Thirty Years War rages between those who think God is physically ailing and those who find the suggestion of fallibility sacrilegious. The New Hundred Years War wages between those who have concluded He never existed in the first place and those who have concluded He is on a romantic junket with his girlfriend.

That's the history. That's why you're under this

defoliating tree now, machine-gun chatter in your ears, your nose aching with Agent Orange, bazooka rounds lighting up the night, clenching the blood-blackened soil in your fingers while the leaves drop around you, loyally crusading for your version of God's nonexistence.

Will-o'-the-Wisp

In the afterlife you are invited to sit in a vast comfortable lounge with leather furniture and banks of television monitors. Upon the millions of blue-green glowing screens, you watch the world unfold. You can control the audio coming through your headphones. With a remote control, you can change the angles of the celestial cameras to capture the right action.

So although you're not a part of life on Earth anymore, you monitor its progress. If you think this could get boring, you're wrong. It is seductive. It is spellbinding. You learn how to watch well. You become invested in the outcome of your descendants' lives. Dozens of intriguing details need to be kept under surveillance. Once you've sat down, the monitors command your attention completely.

In theory, you could choose to watch anything: the private activities of single people in their apartments, the unfolding plans of saboteurs, the detailed progress of battlefields.

But, instead, we all watch for one thing: evidence of our residual influence in the world, the ripples left in our wake. You follow the successes of an organization you started or led. You watch appreciative people read the books you donated to your local religious group. You watch an irrepressible girl with pink shoes climbing the maple tree you planted. These are your fingerprints left on the world; you may be gone, but your mark remains. And you can watch it all.

You may as well get comfortable: the stories play out over long time scales. You may choose to monitor the video screen showing your grandson, an aspiring playwright, deep in thought on a park bench, scribbling notes for a scene. You'll be able to follow him for years to track his success. In the meantime, waitresses drift by you with carts of sandwiches and coffee, and you only need to leave to sleep at night. When you return in the morning, you swipe your membership card at the security gate and choose a nice seat for the day.

But here's the rub: everyone's membership card expires at a different time, and expiration means no more entry into the video lounge. Those who are excluded mill around outside the building, grousing and kicking at the dirt. *Weren't we good?* they ask. *Why should we be locked out while others watch?*

They, too, want to discover how their contributions guide the course of the world, want to see their grandchildren develop, want to witness the proud future of their family name. They grieve and commiserate with one another.

But they don't know the full story. Locked outside, they miss seeing their organizations lose members. They miss watching their favorite people melt away with cancer. They miss seeing the aspiring playwright amount to nothing and do not have to watch his solitary death as he tries to drive himself to the hospital but draws his last ragged breath on the roadside. They miss the drift of social mores, their great-great-grandchildren changing religions, their lines of genetic descent petering out. They don't have to watch as Moses and Jesus and Muhammad go the way of Osiris and Zeus and Thor.

Meanwhile, they kick the dirt and protest. They don't understand they've been blessed with insulation from the future, while the sinners are cursed in the blue-green glow of the televisions to witness every moment of it.

Incentive

Even with the aid of our modern deductive skills, it is impossible to imagine our own death. It is not because we lack insight, but because the concept of death is made up. There is no such thing. This will become clear to you at some point, when you get into a situation that you think should kill you—say, a severe car crash. You'll be surprised to realize that it didn't hurt. The witnesses around you will laugh and help you up and brush off the glass and explain the situation.

The situation is that the people around you are Actors. Your interactions with other people were almost entirely scripted from their point of view. Your "afterlife," if you want to call it that, is your initiation to the game.

We realize this moment of disclosure will be hard on you. *For God's sake*, you will think as you pick yourself up from the car wreck, *what about my lover? What was our relationship based on? Were all the nighttime whispers fabrications? Rehearsed lines? And all my friends: Actors? My parents: pretending?*

Don't despair. It's not as bad as you think. If you think you were the only uninitiated one while all the rest were Actors, you're not quite correct. About half the people are Actors, and the rest, like you until moments ago, are the Beneficiaries. So it is equally likely that your lover was in the same naive boat you were—and now it is your responsibility to become an Actor for her, so that she detects no change in the relationship. You will become like an adulterous spouse striving to force normal behavior. You may have to be an Actor for other Beneficiaries as well: your boss, your cabdriver, your waitress.

As an Actor, you get to see the backs of things. When you finish a conversation with a Beneficiary and exit the room, you find yourself in a backstage waiting area, where slanted two-by-fours hold up the unfinished backs of walls. There are couches here, and you can get snacks from vending machines. You make small talk with other Actors while you wait for your next appearance. Your next appearance will be, say, at 12:53 p.m. for what appears to be a coincidental run-in with someone on the subway.

Before each appearance, you are given a small script on a note card. Generally the instructions are vague. For example, you may be instructed to feign surprise when you run into the Beneficiary; perhaps you will also be instructed to pretend you have just bought a dog or, alternatively, to act as though work is weighing on your mind. Other times the instructions include something quite specific: you are to mention somewhere in the conversation the title of a new book, or drop the name of a mutual friend. Presumably, other Actors during the week will have similar assignments, so the Beneficiary will be guided toward a new idea or meeting.

So you memorize your brief script, and when you

walk back through the door you will be wherever you are next needed: the restaurant bathroom, or the museum gift shop where your friend is waiting to meet you, or perhaps a bustling sidewalk where you are to be spotted arm in arm with another Actor. For the Beneficiaries, the back sides of all doors are constructed just before they enter; for the Actors, all the doors of the world are our portal into and out of this waiting room. We don't know how the Directors dynamically construct the world, much less for what purpose. We are only told that our obligation here as Actors will eventually end, and then we will move on to a better place.

You may decide you're not willing to uphold this continuous lie to the Beneficiaries. You may yell into the Directors' intercom that you won't be their deceitful stool pigeon. This is a typical reaction. But very quickly you will relent and play your part earnestly. We don't know much about the Directors, only that they are clever enough to get us to do something we don't want to do.

Why do we play our parts so earnestly? Why don't we go on strike and blow the cover of the truth? One factor is the sincerity in the face of your lover: her life of unexpected reactive emotion, her heartfelt belief in chance and spontaneity. You're slave to that gorgeous earnestness in her eyes, her engagement with a world of possibility.

But in truth there is a deeper reason you play your part so convincingly. If you play your part well, you can more quickly leave this acting job. Those with the best behavior are rewarded with ignorance: they are reincarnated as an uninitiated Beneficiary. You could permanently blow the cover, but the Directors are confident that you won't; they know you will sink to any depth of infidelity to preserve the lie for your eventual return to it.

Death Switch

There is no afterlife, but a version of us lives on nonetheless.

At the beginning of the computer era, people died with passwords in their heads and no one could access their files. When access to these files was critical, companies could grind to a halt. That's when programmers invented death switches.

With a death switch, the computer prompts you for your password once a week to make sure you are still alive. When you don't enter your password for some period of time, the computer deduces you are dead, and your password is automatically emailed to the second-in-command. Individuals began to use death switches to reveal Swiss bank account numbers to their heirs, to get the last word in an argument, and to confess secrets that were unspeakable during their lifetime.

It soon became appreciated that death switches provided a good opportunity to say good-bye electronically. Instead of sending out passwords, people began programming their computers to send emails to their friends announcing their own death. "It appears I'm dead now," the email would begin. "I'll take this as an opportunity to tell you things I've always wanted to express . . . "

Soon enough, people realized they could program messages to be delivered on dates in the future: "Happy 87th birthday. It's been twenty-two years since my death. I hope your life is proceeding delightfully."

With time, people began to push death switches further. Instead of confessing their death in the emails, they pretended they were not dead at all. Using auto-responder algorithms that cleverly analyzed incoming messages, a death switch could generate apologetic excuses to turn down invitations, to send congratulations on a life event, and to claim to be looking forward to a chance to see someone again soon.

Today, building a death switch to pretend you are not dead has become an art form. Death switches are programmed to send a fax occasionally, make a transfer between bank accounts, or make an online purchase of the latest novel. The most sophisticated switches reminisce about shared adventures, exchange memories about a good escapade, swap inside jokes, brag about past feats, and summon up lifetimes of experience.

In this way, death switches have established themselves as a cosmic joke on mortality. Humans have discovered that they cannot stop Death, but at least they can spit in his drink.

This began as a good-spirited revolution against the grave's silence. The problem for those of us still living, however, is the increasing difficulty in determining who's dead and who's alive. Computers operate around the clock, sending out the social intercourse of the dead: greetings, condolences, invitations, flirtations, excuses, small talk, inside jokes—codes between people who know each other well.

And it is clear now where this society is going. Most people have died off, and we are some of the few remaining. By the time we die and our death switches are triggered, there will be nothing left but a sophisticated network of transactions with no one to read them: a society of emails zipping back and forth under silent satellites orbiting a soundless planet.

So an afterlife does not exist for us per se, but instead an afterlife occurs for that which exists between us. When an alien civilization eventually bumps into Earth, they will immediately be able to understand what humans were about, because what will remain is the network of relationships: who loved whom, who competed, who cheated, who laughed together over road trips and holiday dinners. Each person's ties to bosses, brothers, and lovers are etched into the electronic communiqués. The death switches simulate the society so completely that the entire social network is reconstructable. The planet's memories survive in zeros and ones.

This situation allows us indefinitely to revisit shared jokes, remedy lost opportunities for a kind word, and recall stories about delightful Earthly experiences that can no longer be felt. Memories now live on their own; no one forgets them or grows tired of telling them. We are quite satisfied with this arrangement, because reminiscing about our glory days of existence is perhaps all that would have happened in an afterlife anyway.

Encore

Although the concept of the afterlife is quite old, its full-scale implementation has only gotten into swing in the last century. The afterlife existed before then, but only barely.

To understand this, you need to be aware that your Creators are talented at just that—creation— but they're not involved with the observation and judgment of our actions, as we had previously supposed them to be. The Creators watch none of the details as our lives unfold. They could not care less. Only afterward do they become interested again, when they have the opportunity to do what they do best: create. At this second stage, they are called Re-Creators, and their goal is to find all available records of your life and create a simulation of you, reconstructing all your days. They take it as their challenge to see if they can recover a good likeness of you from the piles of evidence you've left behind.

They begin by tracking down your birth, marriage, and death records. For most people, the afterlife started only a few hundred years ago, when record keeping began. They then take account of the phone company records: every call you made and to whom. Every credit card purchase is retrieved and analyzed for time, location, and purchase. The Re-Creators analyze every existing frame of video footage on the planet for your every appearance: buying coffee at a convenience store, standing in front of an ATM withdrawing money, clutching a diploma, walking unwittingly in the background of other people's home videos, eating a hot dog in the bleachers during a basketball game.

They're artists of information, and each data point adds a bit more pigment to their accumulating portrait of you. Each detail is marked with a confidence rating for the source and checked for consistency against the other data points. Millions of facts are gathered, facts so richly structured and interconnected that they constitute a hard shell that retains your shape when you disappear from the middle of it.

From school records, the Re-Creators closely approximate what pieces of knowledge you had at a particular moment in your life. This information is neatly dovetailed with detailed historical records. They re-create what you were likely to have seen around you each day and, by examining your newspaper subscriptions, they model the world events that would have affected you.

From deep within this jungle of data they can deduce the exact dates of your various relationships: when they began, when they ended, and whether they overlapped. The Re-Creators come to understand you from every form you filled out, every word you typed on the Internet, the mail you received from others: why people thank you, who chastises you, what advice your lovers seek, what favors your friends ask. Which mailing lists you're on. Your tax returns.

In previous generations, when you awoke in the afterlife, it was easy to tell that you were merely a simulation, because your details were so sparse. The feeling of emptiness on most days allowed you to know that you were a cheap reproduction of your former self. But with today's rich data, the Re-Creators can reconstruct you so seamlessly that your afterlife is essentially a perfect replica of the original. It feels so much like the real thing that in the afterlife you only rarely wonder whether you've lived all this before, haunted occasionally by déjà vu, holding a book in your hand and not knowing whether this is the first time or a replay from aeons past.

Prism

God resolved at the outset that He wanted every human to participate in the afterlife. But the plans weren't thought out to completion, and immediately He began to run up against some confusion about age. How old should each person be in the afterlife? Should this grandmother exist here at her age of death, or should she be allowed to live as a young woman, recognizable to her first lover but not to her granddaughter? He decided it was unfair to keep people the age they were at the end of their lives, when much of their beauty and alacrity had been worn down. Allowing everyone to live as a young adult proved an unviable solution because the afterlife quickly degenerated into unbounded sexual pursuits. And at middle ages they talked only about their children and mortgages, making conversations in the afterlife tedious.

God finally landed on an ingenious solution while watching light diffract through a prism. So when you arrive here, you are split into your multiple selves at all possible ages. The *you* that existed as a single identity is now all ages at once. These pieces of you no longer get older but remain ageless into perpetuity. The yous have transcended time.

This takes some getting used to. The different beams of you might run into each other at the grocery store, like separate people do in Earth life. Your seventy-six-year-old self may revisit his favorite creek and run into your eleven-year-old self. Your twenty-eight-year-old self may break up with a lover in a diner, and notice your thirty-five-year-old self visiting that spot, lingering on the air of regret hanging over the empty seat.

Typically the different yous are happy to see each other because they possess the same name and a shared history. But the yous are more critical of yourselves then they are of others, and so each you quickly identifies habits that get under your skin.

It's a fact of afterlife: don't be surprised to discover that after decomposition into your different ages, the different yous tend to drift apart.

You discover that the you of eight years old has less in common than expected with the you of thirty-two and the you of sixty-four. The eighteen-year-old you finds more in common with other eighteen-year-olds than with your seventy-three-year-old you. The seventy-three-year-old you doesn't mind a bit, seeking out meaningful conversations with others of the same generation. Beyond the name, the yous have little else in common.

But don't lose hope: the shared résumé of life—parents, birthplace, hometown, school years, first kiss—has a magnetic, nostalgic pull, so once in a while the different yous organize a gathering, like a family reunion, bringing together all your ages into a single room. At these reunions, the middle-aged will delightedly pinch the cheeks of the young, and the teenagers will politely listen to the stories and advice of the elderly.

These reunions reveal a group of individuals touchingly searching for a common theme. They appeal to your name as a unifying structure, but they come to realize that the name that existed on Earth, the you that moved serially through these different identities, was like a bundle of sticks from different trees. They come to understand, with awe, the complexity of the compound identity that existed on the Earth. They conclude with a shudder that the Earthly you is utterly lost, unpreserved in the afterlife. You were all these ages, they concede, and you were none.

Ineffable

When soldiers part ways at war's end, the breakup of
the platoon triggers the same emotion as the death of
a person—it is the final bloodless death of the war.
This same mood haunts actors on the drop of the
final curtain: after months of working together,
something greater than themselves has just died.
After a store closes its doors on its final evening, or a
congress wraps its final session, the participants
amble away, feeling that they were part of something
larger than themselves, something they intuit had a
life even though they can't quite put a finger on it.

In this way, death is not only for humans but for
everything that existed.

And it turns out that anything which enjoys life
enjoys an afterlife. Platoons and plays and stores and
congresses do not end—they simply move on to a
different dimension. They are things that were created and existed for a time, and therefore by the cosmic rules they continue to exist in a different realm.

Although it is difficult for us to imagine how
these beings interact, they enjoy a delicious afterlife
together, exchanging stories of their adventures.
They laugh about good times and often, just like
humans, lament the brevity of life. The people who

constituted them are not included in their stories. In truth, they have as little understanding of you as you have of them; they generally have no idea you existed.

It may seem mysterious to you that these organizations can live on without the people who composed them. But the underlying principle is simple: the afterlife is made of spirits. After all, you do not bring your kidney and liver and heart to the afterlife with you—instead, you gain independence from the pieces that make you up.

A consequence of this cosmic scheme may surprise you: when you die, you are grieved by all the atoms of which you were composed. They hung together for years, whether in sheets of skin or communities of spleen. With your death they do not die. Instead, they part ways, moving off in their separate directions, mourning the loss of a special time they shared together, haunted by the feeling that they were once playing parts in something larger than themselves, something that had its own life, something they can hardly put a finger on.

Pantheon

There is not a single God but many. Each rules a separate territory. Despite the best guesses of erstwhile civilizations, the gods do not hold dominion over categories of war, love, and wisdom. Instead, the divisions are much finer-grained. One god has control over objects that are made of chrome. Another over flags. Another over bacteria. The god of telephones, the god of bubble gum, the god of spoons: these are the players in an incalculably large panoply of deific bureaucracy.

There is always disputed territory. It is the interaction within this substantial administration that determines the random walk of the world: everything interesting happens at the borders between domains of power.

So while you may be pleased to know that there is, after all, divine intentionality, you may be disappointed to know that no two gods can agree. There are so many that it is difficult for them to enjoy any consequence except during brief statistical hiccups.

Just as the Greeks surmised, there is bitter competition among the gods. Jealous rivalries abound because the stakes are so low; the gods are not large and powerful and they know it. So they try their best to stand out and to be heard, given the limits of their random talents and the cards they are dealt. They discover themselves tossed into a sea of interaction with strangers, struggling for progress in a network of jealous competition. Many of them embrace a suspicion that something extraordinary could happen if they could collaborate on a meaningful scale, but they find themselves continually stymied by the personalized nature of their goals.

Lately it has become popular to theorize that their incapacity to coordinate is the only reason they have not destroyed us. But the truth is that they are fond of us and work to keep us well protected. When they feel overwhelmed by their own struggles, they sit down and observe a traffic jam. They watch how each human driver aims for his own private piece of the city, isolated from neighbors by layers of glass and steel. Some of the humans reach out to make cell phone contact with a single friend out of the innumerable hordes. And gazing out over the steering wheel, each human feels the intensities of joy and grief as though his were the only real examples in the world.

Among all the creatures of creation, the gods favor us: we are the only ones who can empathize with their problems.

Impulse

Just as there is no afterlife for a computer chip, there is none for us: we are, after all, the same thing. Humans are the small networked units of hardware running a massive and unseen software program, the product of three cosmic Programmers. The Programmers are experts in building flexible computational substrates made of nodes—in this case, humans—that are mobile, self-healing, and possess high bandwidth. With every contact between humans, the network crunches through calculations immeasurably large, reconfiguring its colossal circuitry on the fly, computing for beings on a different spatial scale.

The surprise is that all the computational operations run below the surface of our consciousness. So take careful note the next time your neighbor's eyelid produces a single, barely perceptible twitch. Normally neither of you would be conscious of it—but your subconscious brain notices. To those hidden parts of your brain, the detected twitch stimulates a cascade of changes: genes unwrap, proteins blossom, synapses rearrange. All this is well below your awareness—you are merely carrying the brainbox with no acquaintance with what happens inside it. This surge of neural activity causes you immediately to release pheromones that are consciously undetectable but have considerable influence on the nervous system of the young woman sitting next to you: moments later, she unwittingly taps her left foot, once. This is picked up by the brain of the tourist sitting across from her, and onward the computation evolves.

In this manner, all across the vast network of humanity, signals are passed at a blinding pace without any of us knowing we are messengers. The unconscious lifting of a finger to scratch under the rim of a hat, the sudden appearance of gooseflesh, the exact timing of a blink—these all carry information and compel the processing to the next stage. The human race is a gargantuan network of signals passed from node to node, a calculation of celestial significance running on the vast grid of the human substrate.

But it turns out that a tiny, unexpected bug has crept into the program, an anomalous algorithm that the Programmers did not intend and have not yet detected: our consciousness. Everything we adore, abhor, covet, can't bear, take pleasure in, desire, pursue, crave, aspire to, long for—all these run on top of the planetary program, hidden within the thick forests of its code. Love was not specified in the design of your brain; it is merely an endearing algorithm that freeloads on the leftover processing cycles.

The Programmers are as unaware of our conscious lives as we are of their calculations. In theory, they should be able to ascertain a slight drain on the computing resources, even though the calculations would be far too elaborate and tangled for an investigation of the problem. But they have not bothered, because they are thrilled with how things are going. Something has happened here that they do not understand: the computing power of the grid has grown at a blinding pace.

They find this mysterious, for they had engineered the nodes only for zero-growth replacement. Knowing that the humans would eventually wear out, the Programmers had equipped them with a lock-and-key mechanism for self-reproduction when the time came. But they didn't foresee the anomalous algorithm, or how it would accidentally create a deep loneliness in the nodes, a need for companionship, and ongoing sagas of drama and fulfillment. The resultant lovemaking has vastly amplified the size of the grid, growing it rapidly from thousands to billions of nodes. For reasons beyond the Programmers' understanding, the nodes go to heroic lengths to keep themselves alive and turning the locks and keys. Of all the Programmers' planets, ours is the supercomputing golden child, the world that inexplicably provides enough power to light up the galaxy.

Quantum

Here in the afterlife, everything exists in all possible states at once, even states that are mutually exclusive. This comes as a shock after your Earthly life, where making one choice causes the other choices to disappear. When you become a lover to one, you cannot become a lover to others; when you choose one door, others are lost to you.

In the afterlife you can enjoy all possibilities at once, living multiple lives in parallel. You find yourself simultaneously eating and not eating. You are bowling and not bowling at the same time. You are horseback riding and nowhere near a horse.

A velvety blue angel gently descends to see how you are coming along with this afterlife.

"This is all too confusing for a poor human brain," you confess to the angel.

The angel rubs his chin. "Maybe we can ease you into this with something simpler, like a day job," he offers.

You are immediately dropped into a work life of simultaneous contradictions. You are concurrently practicing several careers at once, all the careers you had considered when you were younger. You simultaneously count down your rocket ship launch and defend a criminal client in front of a jury. In the same moments, you scrub your hands for a gallbladder surgery and navigate an eighteen-wheeler down a New Mexico interstate. Gone are the constraints of location and time.

"This," you tell the angel, "is too much work."

"Perhaps we could warm you up with a simpler situation," he considers. "How would you like to be in a closed room, one-on-one with your lover?"

And then you are here. You are simultaneously engaged in her conversation and thinking about something else; she both gives herself to you and does not give herself to you; you find her objectionable and you deeply love her; she worships you and wonders what she might have missed with someone else.

"Thank you," you tell the angel. "This I'm used to."

Conservation

What we have deduced about the Big Bang is almost exactly wrong. Instead of a Big Bang, the genesis of the universe consisted of the uneventful, accidental, hushed production of a single quark.

For thousands of millennia, nothing occurred. The solitary particle floated in silence. Eventually it considered moving. Like all elementary particles, it realized that its direction of travel in time was arbitrary. So it shot forward in time and, looking back, it realized that it had left a single pencil stroke across the canvas of space-time.

It raced back through time in the other direction, and saw that it had left another stroke.

The single quark began to dash back and forth in time, and like the individually meaningless actions of an artist's pencil, a picture began to emerge.

If it feels to you that we're connected by a larger whole, you're mistaken: we're connected by a smaller particle. Every atom in your body is the same quark in different places at the same moment in time. Our little quark sweeps like a frenetic four-dimensional phosphor gun, painting the world: each leaf on every tree, every coral in the oceans, each car tire, every bird carried on the wind, all the hair on all the heads in the world. Everything you have ever seen is a manifestation of the same quark, racing around on a space-time superhighway of its own invention.

It began to write the story of the world with sagas of war, love, and exile. As it spun out stories and allowed the plots to grow organically, the quark became an increasingly talented storyteller. The stories took on subtle dimensions. Its protagonists engaged in moral complexity; its antagonists were charming. The quark reached for inspiration into its own history of loneliness in an empty cosmos: the adolescent with his head on the pillow, the divorcée staring out the coffee shop window, the retiree watching infomercials—these became the prophets of the quark's text.

But the quark did not dwell upon the loneliness. It found that it couldn't get enough of the love stories and the sex scenes. From the complex network of love stories spawned new generations of children, and the storyboard of the space-time canvas became increasingly rich in characters. The quark pursued the logical flow of each story with dedication and integrity.

Then, on an afternoon that would come to be known by our physicists as the Day of Decline, the quark suffered an epiphany. It realized it had reached the limits of its energy. Its stories had grown too baroque and rococo to be contained by the maximum speed of its pencil strokes.

That was the first day the world began drifting toward incompleteness. The quark despondently resigned itself to the fact that it could keep the show going only if it saved energy. It realized it could accomplish this by drawing only those entities that were being observed by someone. Under this conservation program, the great meadows and mountains were only drawn when there was someone there to look. There was nothing drawn under the sea surface where submarines did not travel; there were no jungles where explorers did not probe.

These measures of savings were already in place before you were born. But things are about to get worse. Even with these energy management programs, the quark remains overextended. Given the directionless and explosive growth of the human chronicle, our quark's reserves are nearing depletion.

Soon, against its will, it will submit to the fact that it cannot continue the narrative. The physicists have advised us to prepare ourselves emotionally for the end of our world: trees will have fewer leaves, both men and women will bald, animals will be drawn with less detail. As the decline continues, you will someday turn a familiar corner to find buildings missing. At some point you may look through the missing walls of your bedroom to find your lover only half drawn.

This is the proffered prediction but, fortunately for us, the physicists have slightly miscalculated. Missing from their equations is the fact that the quark loves us too much to allow this to happen. It cares about its creation and knows it would break our hearts to see through the veneer.

So it has a slightly different plan. It will end the world in sleep. All the quark's creatures will curl up where they are. Morning commuters in suits will sink softly into slumber behind their steering wheels. Highways, locomotives, and subways will slow to a muted halt. Office workers will make themselves drowsily comfortable on the floors and hallways of their tall buildings. The squares of the world's capitals will drift into silence. Farmers in their wheat fields will doze off as midflight insects touch down softly like snowflakes. Horses will arrest their gallop and relax into a standing slumber. Black jaguars in trees will lower their chins to their paws on the branches. This is how the world will close, not with a bang but a yawn: sleepy and contented, our own falling eyelids serving as the curtain for the play's end.

This way, the quark's beloved creations will be unable to witness what happens next. What happens next is the world's recession, the unraveling of the planet. As the quark slows, its individual pencil strokes become increasingly sparse until the world resembles a crosshatched woodcut. The sleeping bodies become transparent netting through which the other side can be seen. As the pencil marks grow fewer, the asphalt highways become a sparse lacing of black strokes, with nothing below but the other side of the planet, one Earth-diameter away. The world's canvas devolves into a thin sketch of outlines. The remaining strokes, one by one, disappear from the latticework, drawing the cosmos toward a more complete blankness.

In the end, spent, the quark slows to a halt at the center of infinite emptiness.

Here it takes its time, catching its breath. It will wait several thousand millennia until it regains the stamina and optimism to try again. So there is no afterlife, but instead a long intermission: all of us exist inside the memory of the particle, like a fertilized egg waiting to unpack.

Narcissus

In the afterlife you receive a clear answer about our purpose on the Earth: our mission is to collect data. We have been seeded on this planet as sophisticated mobile cameras. We are equipped with advanced lenses that produce high-resolution visual images, calculating shape and depth from wavelengths of light. The cameras of the eyes are mounted on bodies that carry them around—bodies that can scale mountains, spelunk caves, cross plains. We are out-fitted with ears to pick up air-compression waves and large sensory sheets of skin to collect temperature and texture data. We have been designed with ana-lytic brains that can get this mobile equipment on top of clouds, below the seas, onto the moon. In this way, each observer from every mountaintop con-tributes a little piece to the vast collection of plane-tary surface data.

We were planted here by the Cartographers, whose holy books are what we would recognize as maps. Our calling is to cover every inch of the planet's surface. As we roam, we vacuum data into our sensory organs, and it is for this reason only that we exist.

At the moment of our death we awaken in the debriefing room. Here our lifetime of data collection is downloaded and cross-correlated with the data of those who have passed before us. By this method, the Cartographers integrate billions of viewpoints for a dynamic high-resolution picture of the planet. They long ago realized that the optimal method for achieving a planet-wide map was to drop countless little rugged mobile devices that multiply quickly and carry themselves to all the reaches of the globe. To ensure we spread widely on the surface, they made us restless, longing, lusty, and fecund.

Unlike previous mobile-camera versions, they built us to stand, crane our necks, turn our lenses onto every detail of the planet, become curious, and independently develop new ideas for increased mobility. The brilliance of the design specification was that our pioneering efforts were not prescripted; instead, to conquer the unpredictable variety of landscapes, we were subjected to natural selection to develop dynamic, unforeseen strategies. The Cartographers do not care who lives and dies, as long as there is broad coverage. They are annoyed by worship and genuflection; it slows data collection.

When we awaken in the giant spherical windowless room, it may take a few moments to realize that we are not in a heaven in the clouds; rather, we are deep at the center of the Earth. The Cartographers are much smaller than we are. They live underground and are averse to light. We are the biggest devices they could build: to them we are giants, large enough to jump creeks and scale boulders, an impressive machine ideal for planetary exploration.

The patient Cartographers pushed us out onto a

spot on the surface and watched for millennia as we spread like ink over the surface of the planet until every zone took on the color of human coverage, until every region came under the watchful gaze of the compact mobile sensors.

Estimating our progress from their control center, the mobile camera engineers congratulated themselves on a job well done. They waited for humans to spend lifetimes turning their data sensors on patches of ground, the strata of rocks, the distribution of trees.

And yet, despite the initial success, the Cartographers are profoundly frustrated with the results. Despite their planetary coverage and long life spans, the mobile cameras collect very little that is useful for cartography. Instead, the devices turn their ingeniously created compact lenses directly into the gazes of other compact lenses—an ironic way to trivialize the technology. On their sophisticated sensory skin, they simply want to be stroked. The brilliant air-compression sensors are turned toward the whispers of lovers rather than critical planetary data. Despite their robust outdoor design, they have spent their energies building shelters into which they cluster with one another. Despite good spreading on large scales, they clump at small scales. They build communication networks to view pictures of one another remotely when they are apart.

Day after day, with sinking hearts, the Cartographers scroll through endless reels of useless data. The head engineer is fired. He has created an engineering marvel that only takes pictures of itself.

Seed

Although we credit God with designing man, it turns out He's not sufficiently skilled to have done so. In point of fact, He unintentionally knocked over the first domino by creating a palette of atoms with different shapes. Electron clouds bonded, molecules bloomed, proteins embraced, and eventually cells formed and learned how to hang on to one another like lovebirds. He discovered that by simmering the Earth at the proper distance from the Sun, it instinctively sprouted with life. He's not so much a creator as a molecule tinkerer who enjoyed a stroke of luck: He simply set the ball rolling by creating a smorgasbord of matter, and creation ensued.

He is as impressed by the gorgeous biological results as the rest of us, and He often spends slow afternoons drifting through jungle canopies or along the sea floor, reveling in the unexpected beauty.

When our species stumbled into sentience, we became awed by His lightning-bolt experiments with electricity, His racing cyclones, His explosive fun with volcanoes. These effects generated more awe and perplexity among the beautiful new species than He had expected. He didn't want to accept credit for something He did not deserve, but acclaim was tendered without request. He began to find humans irresistible with their unrestricted love. We quickly became His chosen species.

Like us, He is awestruck when He ponders the perfect symphonies of internal organs, the global weather systems, the curious menagerie of marine species. He doesn't really know how it all works. He's an explorer, curious and smart, seeking the answers. But with enough of our adoration, the temptation overcame: we assumed the creation was planned, and He no longer corrected the mistake.

Recently He has run into an unforeseen problem: our species is growing smarter. While we were once easy to awe, dragging knuckles and gaping at fire, we have replaced confusion with equations. Tricks we used to fall for have been deduced. Physical laws predict the right answers; the intellectual territories we once gave away now convene under the banner of better explanations. We command theories of physics so strange and complex that God gets blood pressure spikes trying to understand them.

This puts God in a tricky situation. Ancient books relate how God unleashed all His wonders on Egypt. He feels a little defensive now, because He doesn't have any more wonders to unleash, and He's increasingly concerned that we would see the strings if He tried. He's in the position of an amateur magician who performs for small children and suddenly has to play to skeptical adults. All this is reflected in the steady decline of attempted miracles in the past millennia. He is too noble to rely on bluffing, and the thought of being caught and revealed as an amateur embarrasses Him. This is why God has increasingly kept a professional distance from His favorite species. As He grew more withdrawn, saints and martyrs filled the vacuum as His marketing team. He's ashamed now that He didn't put a stop to them earlier; instead, he slipped into seclusion as they generated endless chronicles.

But this story has a happy ending. He has recently faced His limitations, and this has brought Him closer to us. Studying our details from His heavenly outpost, He began to understand that His subjects are entirely capable of empathizing with His position. Everywhere He looks He sees positions of strange credit: parents who seed a child's life but have limited control over it; politicians who briefly steer the ship of state into the dimly lit future; enthusiastic lovers who marry without knowing where the commitment will lead. He studies the accidental co-locations that initiate friendships, inventions, pregnancies, business deals, and car accidents. He realizes that everyone is knocking over dominoes willy-nilly: no one knows where it leads.

In the afterlife, in the warm company of His accidental subjects, God now settles in comfortably, like a grandfather who looks down the long holiday table at his progeny, feeling proud, somehow responsible, and a little surprised.

Graveyard of the Gods

Because the afterlife is a form of justice, we may think that it cannot include animals, who are not held responsible for their actions. Thankfully we would be wrong. It would have been a lonely afterlife without animals, and we have discovered the pleasant truth that the hereafter is full of dogs, mosquitoes, kangaroos, and every other creature. After you arrive and look around for a while, it becomes obvious that anything that once existed enjoys a continued existence.

You begin to realize that the gift of immortality applies to things we *created*, as well. The afterlife is full of cell phones, mugs, porcelain knickknacks, business cards, candlesticks, dartboards. Things that were destroyed—cannibalized naval ships, retired computers, demolished cabinetry—all return in full form to enjoy and furnish the hereafter. Contrary to the admonition that we cannot take it with us, anything we create becomes part of our afterlife. If it was created, it survives.

Surprisingly, this rule applies to creations not only material but also mental. So along with the creations that join us in the afterlife are the gods we created. Lonely in a coffee shop you might meet

Resheph, the Semitic god of plague and war. The head of a gazelle grows from his forehead; he gazes wistfully out the window at passersby. In the grocery store aisle you may bump into the Babylonian death god Nergal, the Greek Apollo, or the Vedic Rudra. In the shopping mall you'll spot gods of flames and moons, goddesses of sexual acts and fertility, gods of fallen warhorses and runaway slaves. Despite their incognito clothing, they are typically detected by their gargantuan size and such characteristics as lion heads, multiple arms, or reptilian tails.

They are lonely, in large part because they've lost their audiences. They used to cure disease, act as intermediaries between the living and dead, and dole out crops and protection and revenge for the loyal. Now no one knows their names. They never asked to be born, yet they find themselves ensnared here for eternity. Only rarely is there a local resurgence of belief in an old god, a small clumping of fans, but such bursts are always short-lived. The gods recognize that they are stuck here with their dealt hand of cards: a vengeful personality, fire for eyes, dysfunctional kin, and eternity on their hands.

When you begin to look around, you'll discover thousands of them. The Aztec Mictlantecuhtli, the Chinese Monkey King Sun Wukong, the Norse Odin. In afterlife phone books you can find the Rainbow Serpent of the Aboriginal Australians, the Prussian Zempat, the Wendish Berstuk, the Algonquian Gitche Manitou, the Sardinian Maymon, the Thracian Zibelthiurdos. At a restaurant you might eavesdrop on the still-cold relationship between the Babylonian sea goddess Tiamat and the storm god Marduk who once split her in two. She picks at her food and only gives curt replies to his attempts at conversation.

Some of the gods are related to one another; others have untraceable genealogies. What they have in common is a proclivity to refuse the free housing offered in the afterlife, although no one is sure why. Most likely it is because they are having a difficult time coming to terms with the idea of sinking to the level of their onetime genuflectors.

Instead, at night, lonely and homeless, they cluster in one another's company on the far edge of the city, lying down to sleep in large grassy meadows. If you're interested in history and theology, you'll enjoy walking these fields of gods, this quiet horizontal spectacle of abandoned deities laid in uneven rows to the vanishing point. Here you might run across Bathalang Maykapal of the Tagalogs, and his main enemy, the Lizard God Bakonawa; having no one who cares about their fights anymore, they now share a lonely bottle of wine. Here you see the god of light, Atea, from the Tuamotu Archipelago, and his son Tane, who in his heyday hurled the patricidal lightning bolts of his ancestor Fatu-tiri; now the whole family sits around, their vendettas withered and difficult to reinvigorate. Look: here's the Maori Tāwhirimātea, the god of storms and winds, who spent his lifetime punishing his brother deities for separating his parents, Rangi and Papatuanuku; with no more audience, his winds are spent and he plays cards with his brothers under calm skies. Over there you can see Khonvoum, supreme god of the Bambuti Pygmy, clutching his bow made of two snakes, which he still believes might appear to mortals as a rainbow. Here is the Shinto fire god Kagu-tsuchi, whose birth burned his mother to death; now the only evidence of his former blaze is a light smoky smell.

Like a museum, these fields of gods, this pastoral encyclopedia of mythology, is a testament to human creativity and reification. The old gods are used to watching us here; the new gods are stung by how quickly they slipped from reverence and martyrdom to desertion and tourism.

Although the gods choose to congregate together out here, the truth is that they cannot stand one another. They are confused because they have found themselves here in the afterlife, but they still, deep down, believe they are in charge. They have typically risen to the top because of their aggression, and they still want to claim supremacy over the others. But here they no longer enjoy the peak of a hierarchy; instead, they suffer side by side in a fellowship of abandonment.

There is only one thing they appreciate about this afterlife. Because of their famed vengefulness and creativity in the arts of torture, they find themselves impressed by this version of Hell.

Apostasy

In the afterlife you meet God. To your surprise and delight, She is like no god that humans have conceived. She shares qualities with all religions' descriptions, but commands a deific grandeur that was captured in the net of none. She is the elephant described by blind men: all partial descriptions with no understanding of the whole.

You can see in Her glittering eyes how delighted She is to hand forth the Book of Truth. The Book cleanly addresses your lifetime of questions with no philosophical gaps or loose threads. As you observe Her excitement about revealing this, you begin to suspect that deep down She was afraid that an especially clear-thinking theologian would guess the answer. All the clues were there, and only people's personal backgrounds got in the way. You notice that She feels relief as She watches while people's biases and traditions impede clear theological guessing. It is only because of these cultural blinders that She retains Her enviable position of revealing the universe's great secrets each day as the dead cross over to Her territory in the next dimension.

If these people were able to completely shake their traditions, the claims of their ancestors, the songs of their childhood—She reasons—they would have a decently clear shot at the right answer. And this is why She was always leery of apostates, those who rejected the particulars of their religion in search of something that seemed more truthful. She disliked them because they seemed the most likely to float a correct guess. If you assumed that God is fond of those who hold loyally to their religions, you were right—but probably for the wrong reasons. She likes them only because they are intellectually nonadventurous and will be sure to get the answer just a bit wrong.

Upon their arrival in the afterlife, She divides people into the Apostates on Her left and the Loyals on Her right. The Apostates are put on the down escalator, and only the Loyals remain in Heaven. Each day She welcomes new Loyals from two thousand religions. She watches them study the Book of Truth and waits for it to sink in with a delicious thrill.

But something has gone terribly wrong with Her plan. The truth does not convince. The newly arrived Loyals have an imperturbable capacity to hold the beliefs with which they arrived, a deep reluctance to consider evidence that separates them from their lifelong context. So She finds Herself unappreciated and lonely, wandering in solitude among the infinite cloudscapes of the nonbelieving believers.

Blueprints

We look forward to finding out answers in the after-life. We're in luck. In the afterlife we are granted the ultimate gift of revelation: an opportunity to view the underlying code.

At first we may be shocked to watch ourselves represented as a giant collection of numbers. As we go about our normal business in the afterlife, in our mind's eye we can see the massive landscape of numbers, stretching to sight's limit in all directions. This set of numbers represents every aspect of our lives. Across its vast plains we spot islands of sevens, jungles of threes, branching rivers of zeros. The size and richness are breathtaking.

As you interact with a lover, you can see her numbers as well, and her interactions with yours. She endearingly sticks out her bottom lip for attention, and your numbers cascade into acrobatics. Digits flip their values like waterfalls. As a result, your eyes lock on to hers, and amorous words form on your lips and travel from your throat in air-compression waves. As she processes the words, her numbers flip, waves of change rippling through her system. She returns your affection, as dictated by the state of her numbers.

My goodness, you realize on your first afternoon here: *This is totally deterministic. Is love simply an operation of the math?*

After watching enough code, a new notion of agency and responsibility dawns. You watch and understand all the signals that lead to a driver stomping on her brakes as her numbers are changed by the numbers of the cat walking in front of the wheels; you can even see the code of the fleas that leap off when the cat leaps. Whether the cat is struck or not struck, you now understand, was not in anyone's control; it was all in the numbers, married together in a gorgeous inevitability. But we also come to understand that the network of numbers is so dense that it transcends simple notions of cause and effect. We become open to the wisdom of the flow of the patterns.

If you assume this gift of revelation is received in Heaven, you're only half right; it is also the punishment designed for you in Hell. The Rewarders originally thought to offer it as a gift, but the Punishers quickly decided they could leverage it as a kind of affliction, drying up life's pleasures by revealing their bloodlessly mechanical nature.

Now the Rewarders and Punishers are in a battle to determine which of them gets more benefit out of this tool. Will humans appreciate the knowledge or be tortured by it?

The next time you are pursuing a new lover in the afterlife, perhaps sharing a bottle of wine after what appeared to be a chance encounter, don't be surprised if both a Rewarder and a Punisher sneak up behind you. The Rewarder whispers into one of your ears, *Isn't it wonderful to understand the code?* The Punisher hisses into your other ear, *Does understanding the mechanics of attraction suck all the life out of it?*

Such a scene is typical of the afterlife, and illustrates how much both parties have overestimated us. This game always ends in disappointment for both sides, who are freshly distraught to learn that being let into the secrets behind the scenes has little effect on our experience. The secret codes of life—whether presented as a gift or a burden—go totally unappreciated. And once again the Rewarder and the Punisher skulk off, struggling to understand why knowing the code behind the wine does not diminish its pleasure on your tongue, why knowing the inescapability of heartache does not reduce its sting, why glimpsing the mechanics of love does not alter its intoxicating appeal.

Subjunctive

In the afterlife you are judged not against other people, but against yourself. Specifically, you are judged against what you could have been. So the afterworld is much like the present world, but it now includes all the yous that could have been. In an elevator you might meet more successful versions of yourself, perhaps the you that chose to leave your hometown three years earlier, or the you who happened to board an airplane next to a company president who then hired you. As you meet these yous, you experience a pride of the sort you feel for a successful cousin: although the accomplishments don't directly belong to you, it somehow feels close.

But soon you fall victim to intimidation. These yous are not really you, they are better than you. They made smarter choices, worked harder, invested the extra effort into pushing on closed doors. These doors eventually broke open for them and allowed their lives to splash out in colorful new directions. Such success cannot be explained away by a better genetic hand; instead, they played your cards better. In their parallel lives, they made better decisions, avoided moral lapses, did not give up on love so easily. They worked harder than you did to correct their mistakes and apologized more often.

Eventually you cannot stand hanging around these better yous. You discover you've never felt more competitive with anyone in your life.

You try to mingle with the lesser yous, but it doesn't assuage the sting. In truth, you have little sympathy for these less significant yous and more than a little haughtiness about their indolence. "If you had quit watching TV and gotten off the couch you wouldn't be in this situation," you tell them, when you bother to interact with them at all.

But the better yous are always in your face in the afterlife. In the bookstore you'll see one of them arm in arm with the affectionate woman whom you let slip away. Another you is browsing the shelves, running his fingers over the book he actually finished writing. And look at this one jogging past outside: he's got a much better body than yours, thanks to a consistency at the gym that you never kept up.

Eventually you sink into a defensive posture, seeking reasons why you would not want to be so well behaved and virtuous in any case. You grudgingly befriend some of the lesser yous and go drinking with them. Even at the bar you see the better yous, buying rounds for their friends, celebrating their latest good choice.

And thus your punishment is cleverly and automatically regulated in the afterlife: the more you fall short of your potential, the more of these annoying selves you are forced to deal with.

Search

In the moment of transition between life and death, only one thing changes: you lose the momentum of the biochemical cycles that keep the machinery running. In the moment before death, you are still composed of the same thousand trillion trillion atoms as in the moment after death—the only difference is that their neighborly network of social interactions has ground to a halt.

At that moment, the atoms begin to drift apart, no longer enslaved to the goals of keeping up a human form. The interacting pieces that once constructed your body begin to unravel like a sweater, each thread spiraling off in a different direction. Following your last breath, those thousand trillion trillion atoms begin to blend into the earth around you. As you degrade, your atoms become incorporated into new constellations: the leaf of a staghorn fern, a speckled snail shell, a kernel of maize, a beetle's mandible, a waxen bloodroot, a ptarmigan's tail feather.

But it turns out your thousand trillion trillion atoms were not an accidental collection: each was labeled as composing *you* and continues to be so wherever it goes. So you're not gone, you're simply taking on different forms. Instead of your gestures being the raising of an eyebrow or a blown kiss, now a gesture might consist of a rising gnat, a waving wheat stalk, and the inhaling lung of a breaching beluga whale. Your manner of expressing joy might become a seaweed sheet playing on a lapping wave, a pendulous funnel dancing from a cumulonimbus, a flapping grunion birthing, a glossy river pebble gliding around an eddy.

From your present clumped point of view, this afterlife may sound unnervingly distributed. But in fact it is wonderful. You can't imagine the pleasure of stretching your redefined body across vast territories: ruffling your grasses and bending your pine branch and flexing an egret's wings while pushing a crab toward the surface through coruscating shafts of light. Lovemaking reaches heights it could never dream of in the compactness of human corporality. Now you can communicate in many places along your bodies at once; you weave your versatile hands over your lover's multiflorous figure. Your rivers run together. You move in concert as interdigitating creatures of the meadow, entangled vegetation bursting from the fields, caressing weather fronts that climax into thunderstorms.

Just as in your current life, the downside is that you are always in flux. As creatures degrade and your fruits fall and rot, you become capable of new gestures and lose others. Your lover might drift away from you in the migratory flight of tropic birds, a receding stampede of wintering elk, or a creek that quietly pokes its head under the ground and pops up somewhere unknown to you.

Many of your same problems apply: temptation, anguish, anger, distrust, vice—and don't forget the dread arising from free choice. Don't be fooled into believing that plants grow mechanically toward the sun, that birds choose their direction by instinct, that wildebeest migrate by design: in fact, everything is seeking. Your atoms can spread, but they cannot escape the search. A wide distribution does not shield you from wondering how best to spend your time.

Once every few millennia, all your atoms pull together again, traveling from around the globe, like the leaders of nations uniting for a summit, converging for their densest reunion in the form of a human. They are driven by nostalgia to regroup into the tight pinpoint geometry in which they began. In this form they can relish a forgotten sense of holiday-like intimacy. They come together to search for something they once knew but didn't appreciate at the time.

The reunion is warm and heartening for a while, but it isn't long before they begin to miss their freedom. In the form of a human the atoms suffer a claustrophobia of size: gestures are agonizingly limited, restricted to the foundering of tiny limbs. As a condensed human they cannot see around corners, they can only talk within short distances to the nearest ear, they cannot reach out to touch across any meaningful expanses. We are the moment of least facility for the atoms. And in this form, they find themselves longing to ascend mountains, wander the seas, and conquer the air, seeking to recapture the limitlessness they once knew.

Reversal

There is no afterlife, but that doesn't mean we don't get to live a second time.

At some point the expansion of the universe will slow down, stop, and begin to contract, and at that moment the arrow of time will reverse. Everything that happened on the way out will happen again, but backward. In this way our life neither dies nor disintegrates, but rewinds.

In this reverse life you are born of the ground. At funeral ceremonies, we dig you up from the earth and transport you grandly to the mortuary, where the birth makeup is removed. You then are taken to the hospital, where, surrounded by doctors, you open your eyes for the first time. In your daily life, broken vases reassemble, meltwater freezes into snowmen, broken hearts find love, rivers flow uphill. Marriages reride rocky roads and eventually end in erotic dating. The pleasures of a lifetime of intercourse are relived, culminating in kisses instead of sleep. Bearded men become smooth-faced children who are sent to schools to gently strip away the original sins of knowledge; reading, writing, and mathematics are expunged. After this diseducation, graduates shrink and crawl and lose their teeth, achieving the purity of the highest state of the infant. On their last day, howling because it is the end of their lives, babies climb back into the wombs of their mothers, who eventually shrink and climb back into the wombs of *their* mothers, and so on like concentric Russian dolls.

In this reverse life you have blissful expectations about what will come next as you experience your story backward. At the moment of reversal you are genuinely happy, for while life must be lived forward the first time, you suspect it will really be understood only upon replay.

But you have a painful surprise in store. You discover that your memory has spent a lifetime manufacturing small myths to keep your life story consistent with who you thought you were. You have committed to a coherent narrative, misremembering little details and decisions and sequences of events. On the way back, the cloth of that story line unravels. Reversing through the corridors of your life, you are battered and bruised in the collisions between reminiscence and reality. By the time you enter the womb again, you understand as little about yourself as you did your first time here.

About the Author

David Eagleman is a neuroscientist and a writer.

A Note on the Type

The text of this book was composed in Apollo, the first typeface ever originated specifically for film composition. Designed
by Adrian Frutiger and issued by the Monotype Corporation
of London in 1964, Apollo is not only a versatile typeface suit-
able for many uses but also pleasant to read in all of its sizes.

Composed by Textech Brattleboro, Vermont
Printed and bound by Thomson-Shore, Dexter, Michigan
Designed by Soonyoung Kwon